ASSUMING THE FORM OF A BUFFALO, MAHISHA CHARGED FORTH SNORTING AND BELLOWING.

HE TRAMPLED UPON DURGA'S MEN...

...AND LASHED AT THEM WITH HIS TAIL.

ENRAGED, DURGA FLUNG A NOOSE AT HIM.

LATER HE ASSUMED THE FORM OF AN ELEPHANT AND TUGGED AT DURGA'S MOUNT WITH HIS TRUNK.

DURGA LOPPED OFF THE TRUNK WITH HER SWORD.

MAHISHA AGAIN ASSUMED THE FORM OF A BUFFALO AND SNORTED WITH RAGE.

TALES OF DURGA

MAHISHA STRUGGLED TO FREE HIMSELF. AS HALF OF HIM EMERGED FROM THE MOUTH OF THE BUFFALO, DURGA RAISED HER SWORD.

THE NEXT MOMENT, MAHISHA FELL DEAD, AT THE FOOT OF DURGA. THE DEVAS WERE OVERJOYED.

O DURGA, UPHOLDER OF VIRTUE, DESTROYER OF EVIL, WE HUMBLY SALUTE YOU! O DEVI, CONTINUE TO PROTECT US!

CHAMUNDI

ON ANOTHER OCCASION, THE DEVAS WERE DRIVEN OUT OF HEAVEN BY SHUMBHA, THE LORD OF THE ASURAS.

CHANDA AND MUNDA, SHUMBHA'S COMMANDERS, FOLLOWED THE DEVAS.

LET'S FIND OUT WHERE THEY GO AND WHY.

THE DEVAS WENT TO MOUNT HIMAVAT AND PRAYED TO DURGA.

O DURGA, PROTECTOR OF THE VIRTUOUS, DESTROY THE EVIL SHUMBHA AND RESTORE RIGHTEOUSNESS.

*AN INCARNATION OF DURGA

HOW DURGA SLEW SHUMBHA

WHEN SHUMBHA LEARNED THAT CHANDA AND MUNDA HAD BEEN KILLED, HE CAME IN PERSON TO DEAL WITH AMBIKA. HIS HUGE ARMY SURROUNDED AMBIKA AND KALI.

THEN THE SHAKTIS — THE INNER FORCE OF VARIOUS GODS — ISSUED FORTH ASSUMING FEMALE FORMS.* OUT OF BRAHMA EMERGED BRAHMANI...

* EACH OF THESE FORMS IS CONSIDERED TO BE AN INCARNATION OF DURGA

VAISHNAVI FOUGHT WITH THE DISCUS, MAHESHWARI WITH THE TRIDENT, AND VARIOUS OTHER SHAKTIS WITH THEIR RESPECTIVE WEAPONS. UNABLE TO FACE THIS ONSLAUGHT, THE ASURAS BEGAN TO FLEE.

FLEEING FROM WOMEN! SHAME ON YOU! TURN ROUND AND FIGHT.

IT WAS THE TERRIBLE ASURA, RAKTABEEJA.

AS RAKTABEEJA RUSHED FORTH, INDRA'S SHAKTI STRUCK HIM WITH HER THUNDERBOLT.

AS EACH DROP OF THE BLOOD FLOWING FROM HIS WOUND TOUCHED THE GROUND...

...THERE ROSE A MIGHTY ASURA, HIS EXACT REPLICA...

...TO FIGHT THE SHAKTIS.

AS THE SHAKTIS WOUNDED EACH OF THE ASURAS THUS BORN, OUT OF HIS BLOOD ROSE MANY MORE ASURAS...

THEN TO THE AMAZEMENT OF SHUMBHA, THE VARIOUS SHAKTIS MERGED INTO DURGA.

SEIZING DURGA, SHUMBHA ROSE INTO THE SKY.

AFTER A FIERCE BATTLE IN MID-AIR, DURGA FLUNG THE ASURA DOWN...

...AND SLEW HIM WITH HER SPEAR. REJOICING, THE DEVAS HEADED BY INDRA APPEARED ON THE SCENE.

WE SALUTE YOU, O MOTHER DURGA, DESTROYER OF EVIL.

Couldn't find the **Amar Chitra Katha** title you wanted in the store next door?

Log on to **www.theackshop.com** where ALL the titles are just a click away

90 million copies of over 400 titles sold in the last 40 years